Once upon a time on the edge of a big, dark forest, there lived a girl called Goldilocks. You've probably heard of her — if so, you will know these three things:

She was small.

Her hair was all golden curls.

And she looked like one of those very good children who never ever seem to get into any trouble. . . .

Well, the truth is, Goldilocks did get into trouble — quite a lot in fact — not because she was bad, but because her curiosity always got the better of her.

Now, a little curiosity can be a wonderful thing, but too much and you have trouble.

And Goldilocks had a little more than too much.

Her mother often worried about letting Goldilocks out of her sight, but sometimes the little girl would ask just one too many questions and stick her fingers in one too many pots of honey and peek under the lid of one too many saucepans. And her mother, unable to bear it any longer, would send her out to collect firewood.

This was just such a morning, and as Goldilocks slipped through the gate, her mother called after her, "Remember these three things.

Do not stray from the path,

be back in time for breakfast,

and whatever you do – make sure you look after your little red shoes."

"Oh I will, Mother," called Goldilocks. And she meant it – well, the bit about her little red shoes anyway.

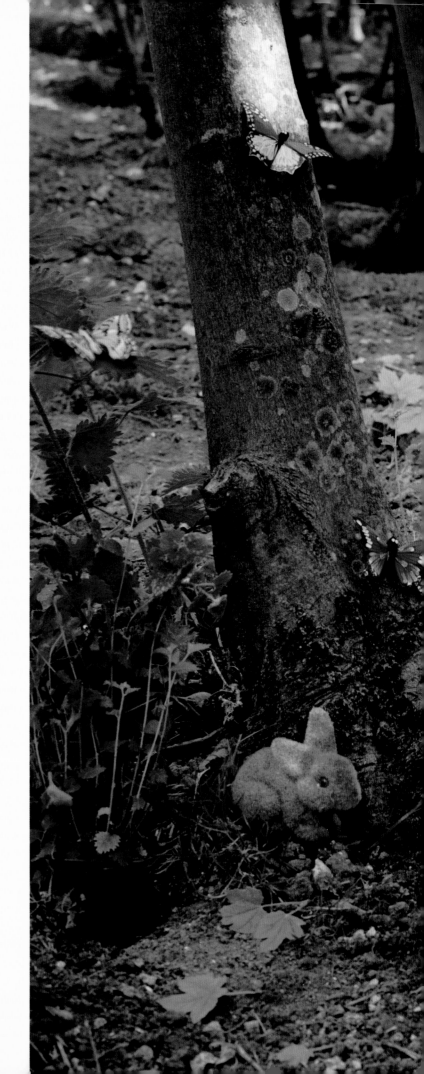

OFF Goldilocks skipped, picking
a flower here and looking down
a rabbit hole there, lifting up pebbles
and peering into tree trunks. But all the
while she remembered her mother's
words and she stuck to the path . . .
well, at least until she saw a little blue
bird pick up a snow-white feather
and fly off into the trees.

Oh, thought Goldilocks, I wonder
where he is going with that feather.
She couldn't help herself – and she
ran through the forest after him.

So intent was she on following the bird
that she didn't notice how far she
had run, nor how thick the trees had
become, until the bird was long gone
and the path was well and truly lost.

Goldilocks stood all alone in the
middle of the forest.

ALL Goldilocks could hear was the leaves rustling and the birds chirping and . . . well . . . something *buzzing*.

I wonder who is making that noise, she thought. And she followed the buzzing until she came to a clearing where the sun shone down.

There, right in the middle of the trees, stood a curious wooden cottage and next to it, three little wooden beehives, each of them surrounded by lots of buzzing bees.

How strange to find a cottage right in the middle of the forest. I *wonder* why I have never seen this cottage before, thought Goldilocks, stretching up to peep through the tiny glass window.

She had to stand on tiptoe and even then she couldn't quite see, so she climbed up onto a flowerpot and her shoes got all muddy.

"Oh, dear," said Goldilocks. "I said I would look after my little red shoes — perhaps whoever lives in this house would help me clean them."

So she knocked on the door. There was no answer, so she peeped through the keyhole.

"No one would mind if I had a look. *I* wouldn't mind if it were *my* house."

So she turned the handle and slipped inside.

"Hello," called out goldilocks. "Hello, hello?" But no one answered, and Goldilocks smiled because she secretly hoped no one would be in.

"What a tidy little room," said Goldilocks out loud and, as she said so, she bumped into a bucket of apples, which tumbled onto the floor.

She didn't have a chance to pick them up because something *rather* curious had caught her eye.

"How strange," she said, stepping over the apples.
"There seem to be three of everything.
There are one, two, three chairs
and one, two, three bowls
and one, two, three spoons
and so one, two, three *people* must live
in this little house."

WELL, she was almost right. You see, the tiny cottage did not belong to one, two, three *people*, but surprisingly, if you don't already know it, one, two, three *bears*.

A large father bear,

a middle-sized mother bear,

and a small baby bear.

I know it's strange to find bears living in a little wooden cottage, but this *is* a fairy tale, and strange things happen in fairy tales.

Every morning the three bears liked to go for a little walk before breakfast. It really gave them an appetite, and it also gave their porridge a chance to cool down—bears do *not* like to burn their tongues.

The bears never bothered to lock their front door because who would walk into a bear's house uninvited? Well, the answer is . . . someone who didn't know it was a bear's house.

THE porridge smelled **very** good, and Goldilocks *was* feeling rather hungry. She looked at the table and she looked at the door and she looked at the porridge.

"**One** little taste would not be so bad – they won't even notice, not a taste from this **large bowl**." And picking up the **biggest** spoon, she dipped it into the **biggest** bowl. "*Ouch!*" she cried. "*Too hot*.

"Maybe this **middle-sized bowl** will be nicer. *Oh no*," said Goldilocks, "*too cold*. How can **anyone** eat cold porridge?

"Perhaps if I just tried this little smaller bowl – that might be better."

And it was—in fact it was *just* **right**. In fact it was **so** just right that she had **another** bite and **another**, until – oh dear – it was **all gone**.
    "Oops," said Goldilocks. "Well, never mind, there are **two** *more* bowls. They can share. *I* would share if it were *my* porridge."

"Hmm," said Goldilocks, looking around the room. "I wouldn't mind a little sit-down. I feel *rather* full.

"What a big chair – I would like to sit on that chair." But she didn't like it at all. "Too tall, too wobbly.

"Well, maybe I will sit on the middle-sized chair" – she sat down with a thud – "*Ouch, too low!*

"Well, that small chair is sweet and more *my* size," said Goldilocks, as she sat down on the smallest chair. "Oh, this is *just* perfect for me."

But it wasn't, and the chair broke into three pieces.

"Oh, dear," said Goldilocks. "Well, it was an accident. I don't suppose anyone would mind if they knew it was an accident."

As GOLDILOCKS PICKED HerseLF up off the floor, she caught sight of the twisty wooden stairs. "Stairs. I *wonder* why I didn't notice those before."

The answer is because she was too busy eating other people's porridge and breaking other people's furniture to have possibly noticed the little staircase winding up through the house.

"Now, I *wonder* what is up there," she whispered.

Well, I think she knew very well what was up there, because most people do – but you see, Goldilocks just wanted to see for herself.

And so she climbed the stairs three at a time, snagging her stripy woolen stockings as she went.

I am sure you will not be surprised to hear that at the top of the stairs she found a bedroom, and in that bedroom were **three** neatly made beds covered in **three** neat quilts, with **three** plump feather pillows.

"What a dear little room," she said, looking around. "If this were *my* house I would sleep in that **big bed**."

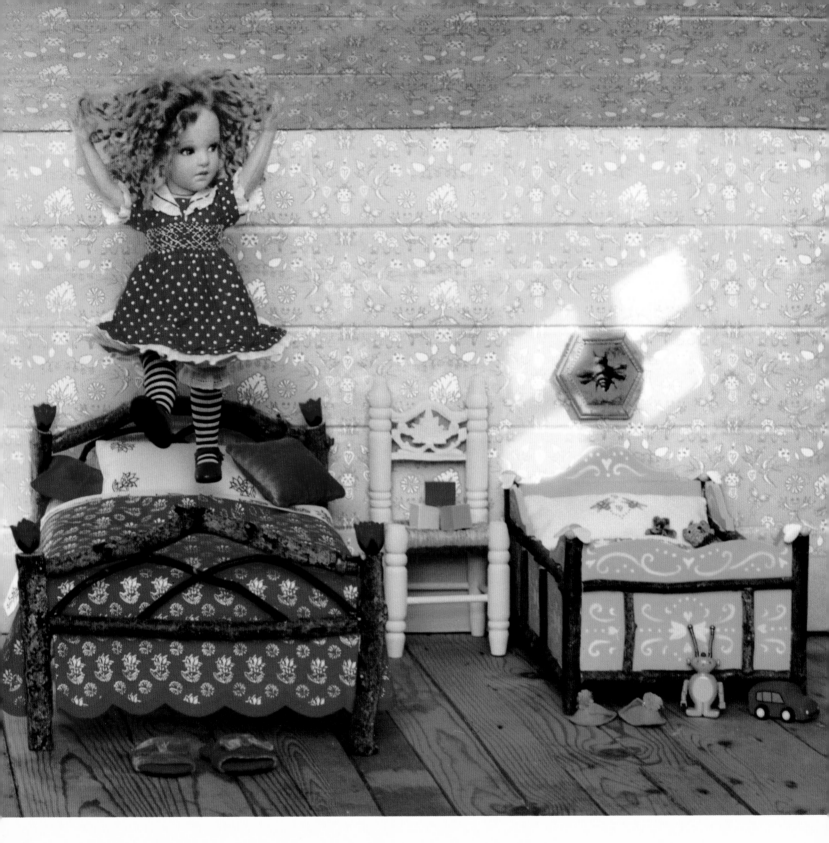

But it wasn't as comfortable as it looked. *"Oh, too hard!"* complained Goldilocks.

You'd think she would have learned by now.

"Well, maybe this middle-sized bed will be more bouncy."

And it was, but it was too bouncy and made her feel a little dizzy.

"Hmm, too soft. I suppose that little bed might be the one for me."

ND as I am sure you have already guessed, it was.

"Oh yes, *just* right," said Goldilocks, slipping under the covers.

"I am so terribly, terribly sleepy – maybe I will lie down, just for three minutes. I'd better take my shoes off though," she said, noticing the mud that she had quite forgotten to clean off.

So Goldilocks carefully placed her little red shoes neatly by the side of the bed and fell soundly asleep.

WHEN the three bears came back from their walk they were very, **very hungry**.

They all sniffed the air – but it **wasn't** porridge they could smell. You see, **bears** have **very** keen noses, and right away they could sniff a *very* **different** smell.

Sniff

Sniff

Sniff

They looked around.

Father Bear noticed at **once** that something was **quite** wrong.

"Things are *not* as they should be," he said, picking up an apple.

FATHER BEAR WALKED OVER to the table and looked into his bowl. He picked up his spoon. "Who has been eating my porridge?"

"Hmm," said Mother Bear. "Who has been eating *my* porridge?"

"Oh," said Small Bear. "Who has been eating *my* porridge? . . . And look – they've gobbled it all up!"

A large tear welled up in Small Bear's eye and rolled down his little face. He was a sensitive type and also very fond of porridge.

F ATHER Bear looked around to see if he could see where the *greedy* whoever-it-was might be, but what he saw was his chair – and he wasn't too pleased.

"Who has been sitting in my chair?"
Father Bear did *not* like people sitting in his chair.

Mother Bear looked at her chair and was not very pleased either.
"Who has been sitting in *my* chair?"

And Small Bear was the least pleased of them all because he no longer even *had* a chair.
"Who has been sitting in *my* chair?
And look, they have broken it all into pieces!"

MOTHER Bear looked around and what she saw was a thread of black wool winding up the stairs. "Things are *not* as they should be," said Mother Bear, picking up the end of the woolen thread.

The **three** bears started to climb the stairs.

Creak

Creak

Creak

But Goldilocks didn't stir, not even a lock of her golden hair, so soundly was she sleeping.

WHEN the bears got to the top of the stairs they listened carefully – bears have **very** sensitive ears – but all they could hear was a tiny, tiny sound almost like the sound of a sleeping mouse.

Father Bear looked at his bed. "Who has been sleeping in my bed?" he snarled.

Mother Bear looked at her bed – the quilt was all ruffled and the pillow unplumped. "Who has been sleeping in *my* bed?" she growled.

"Well," whispered Small Bear, "who has been sleeping in *my* bed?

And

by

the

way . . .

"…look, they are *still* here!"

And all three bears peered at the sleeping girl lying in Small Bear's bed.

Growl

Growl

Growl

And *exactly* then, Goldilocks woke from her slumber to see three differently sized bears staring down at her.

Now, Goldilocks was a curious girl, but she wasn't curious enough to strike up a conversation with bears.

No, no, no!

GOLDILOCKS sprang from the bed and, quick as quick, jumped out of the tiny open window – happily for her it wasn't too big a drop –

and she ran

and she ran

and she ran

as fast as she could, back to her cottage on the edge of the forest.

I can tell you her mother *wasn't* too pleased because she had missed breakfast – not that Goldilocks minded because she was still quite full of porridge. And she was *so* relieved to be home in one piece that she didn't *even* mind being sent to her room.

But she had forgotten two little things.

TWO

little

red shoes.

When her mother realized this, she was extremely cross, as you might imagine. And Goldilocks was very sad because she loved her little red shoes. But Small Bear—well, he was *very* happy indeed.

Mother Bear made him some more porridge, Father Bear mended his chair, and Small Bear had an *almost* brand-new pair of little red shoes to wear when he went for his walk before breakfast.

And Small Bear
looked after them
very carefully indeed.